DINER ROVERS OF THE MILKY WAY

TYLER TORK

Published by Water Dragon Publishing
waterdragonpublishing.com

Experience our other Dragon Gems titles
waterdragonpublishing.com/dragon-gems

ISBN 978-1-967547-90-6 (Trade Paperback)

FIRST EDITION

10 9 8 7 6 5 4 3 2 1

DINER ROVERS OF THE MILKY WAY

"**I**F I HAD A PAYDAY LIKE THAT, I'd buy a house trailer and travel until the money ran out."

Wendy Wilks looked up from her textbook. Hunny Redbone, the waitress at Big Mike's Good Grub and Better Pie, was talking across the counter to the other waitress, Milda something. Afternoon sun slanted in through the big plate-glass windows.

"Then what?" Milda said. "You'd just have to take the same kind of job again. If I had that much money, I'd go to college."

The diner was empty but for them. The cook was in back somewhere, probably napping. Wendy had stretched one cup of coffee and a piece of apple pie into its third hour and was ready for a break from studying. "Good choice," she said, setting her book aside. "I can't understand women who only want to marry and let a man support them, after the War showed we can do every job men have been doing."

"Oh, I still want to marry," Milda said. "But I hear college is a good place to meet men."

Wendy made a face. "What are we talking about, anyway?" She pushed her cup down the counter for her fourth or fifth refill. "Where's all this money coming from?"

Hunny pointed over her shoulder at the radio up on a shelf, permanently tuned to polka station WDUZ in Green Bay, the only station that came in clearly. "They said on the news there's two Visitors flying around eating at restaurants and paying with Lute-something."

"Lutetium?" A lot of the alien Visitors used rare elements for currency.

"Yeah. The smallest bar is worth maybe $10,000, and they don't wait around for change. Nobody knows where they'll show up next, so it might just as well be here."

"I did hear about that, now you mention it." One of the articles the clipping service had sent the university's newly minted Department of Extraterrestrial Studies.

Milda headed for the kitchen with her bin of dishes. "They were on the Movietone News a couple weeks ago, too."

"There's film? Of them, or just people talking about them?"

"Of them." Hunny laughed. "See her perk up! I forgot, you're studying the Visitors, aren't you?"

Milda paused in the kitchen door. "Are you? I thought you were going for chef."

Now Wendy was embarrassed that she didn't remember the last name of someone who remembered her career plans from way back in high school. "I needed to learn French for that, and it turned out I like learning languages and cultures better than cooking. I still cook for friends, but the Visitors are much more interesting." No need to mention that she'd also found that the best cooking schools wouldn't even consider applications from women.

Milda started the water running in the kitchen before reappearing in the pass-thru window. "So Hunny, if they come here, why do you think we'd get that money instead of Big Mike?"

"That's how it works, right?" Hunny sounded truculent. "Any extra money on the table is a tip."

Wendy sipped at her coffee. "Good point. Still, it's unlikely they'll come here. There are a lot of restaurants in the world."

"Hush up," Hunny said. "A girl can dream."

Milda came back out, wiping her hands on her apron. "We should have an agreement, in case they do come. If Mike is here, he'll serve them himself, then claim it was *his* tip. And even if it's just us girls, I wouldn't want us fighting over who gets the table."

"I'd be too terrified to serve them, anyway." Hunny thought for a few seconds. "Let's say we'll split all tips over ten dollars among everyone working tables. If we don't explain why, Mike would go along. Then if they come, he's already agreed how it goes. And since he's not a waitress, he doesn't get a share."

Wendy laughed and started collecting her things. "Hunny, you're the one who should go to college. You'd make a terrific lawyer. Good luck, girls! See you tomorrow!"

Three doors down, the marquee of the recently renamed Saucer Cinema read, "*Ace in the Hole* starring Kirk Douglas & Jan Sterling." As she walked past, the guy in the ticket booth looked up from his comic book and smiled at her. Howard Freleng, another familiar face from high school. Wendy paused. They could get the Movietone footage directly from the company, but that would take weeks. If the newsreel was recent, there was a decent chance there was still a copy in this very building. Wendy put on a smile and approached the ticket window.

Howard spoke first, leaning forward to speak through the grill. "Miss Wilkes, what a delight. Haven't seen you since I got back from Europe. Heard you'd left for college."

"That's true, but it's not far so I visit often. I just don't come into town much." Until this summer, when sister Greta's twins made the house too noisy for study. "I'm pursuing a doctorate at Lawrence, in Appleton."

Howard whistled. "*Doctor* Wilks."

"Someday."

"The next show starts in an hour. Come in and visit till then, if you like."

"Actually, I'm here for a different reason. I wonder whether I might ask a favor."

●　　　●　　　●

It was four miles by bicycle to Hilbert, where Wendy's brother was helping co-ordinate the entertainment at the third annual Cheese Derby picnic. Tad acknowledged her with a nod as she pulled up beside the bandstand, but waited until the band finished their number before wandering over, chewing on a weed. "What do you think, sis? Will they make Carnegie Hall?"

"No, but they have lots of energy, and all finished at more or less the same time. And of course, their uniforms are excellent." That was Tad's department.

"Very true. What's up? If you're tired of studying, Mrs. Gunderson could use a hand with the bunting."

"I need a ride into Appleton."

He nodded. "Greta's ankle-biters finally pushed you over the edge? I'm not surprised. Give them a couple of years and they'll be outside torturing the ducks, instead of running around the house like wild Indians. Okay, in about an hour and a half I can run you into town. But you'll miss the many delights of the Derby. We have a dunking booth this year, where you can submerge many local notables. I'm performing magic on Saturday evening. And the cheeses, of course ..." He shrugged.

Wendy smiled. "I'll try to make it back for the festivities, I promise. It's a school thing."

"I won't stand in the way of your education. But Mrs. Gunderson really could use some help, if you have time until I'm free."

"Of course."

•　　　•　　　•

Wendy rolled down the car window to let air into Tad's sweltering hand-me-down Packard. As they got onto the highway, they passed a few faded billboards—Pepsi, Chevrolet, Chesterfields. "What's your plan, after the festival?"

Tad glanced at her warily. "There's the hay to get in ..."

"Which they can perfectly well do without you, now that John's there to help. You're out of high school two years now. Do you really want to be a farmer? I don't think country life suits you."

"No, I'd like to move, probably to Madison. I'm sure I can find theatre work there. I have a little money saved up."

"There's no reason to wait." He'd be safer there, too, but that wasn't something they could talk about. Wendy stared out the window as another mile went by. "What if you had more than a little money? Say five thousand dollars, what would you do then?"

"Same thing, but in New York City. Why, did you come into a windfall you'd like to share? Or are you proposing we rob a bank?"

"No. The girls at the diner were just dreaming big dreams."

"Hmph. What about you?"

"What would I do?" Wendy thought about it. "I don't know. I'm pretty happy now."

"*Please* don't tell me you'd leave it in the bank."

"Who do you think you're talking to? Probably, until I finish my degree. Then I'd use it to travel and study the Visitors. If they ever settle down anywhere. I want to be the one who cracks their languages."

•   •   •

The entire department—which was to say Dr. Dinkins, Wendy, and Ben Forrest, the other doctoral student, met in an empty classroom to watch the newsreel.

The segment on the Visitors was only ninety seconds of a ten-minute reel. They'd turned up at a diner near a

New York television studio, and Wendy could imagine people running over to let them know, cameramen grabbing whatever camera was most portable, to rush down the block to Soderberg's Delicatessen.

The two Visitors had already been at a table when the news crew caught up with them. They gave brief, unreadable looks before returning to their menus. The place was empty but for a few customers at distant tables keeping a careful eye on the Visitors—presumably everyone else had cleared out. The announcer treated the story as a joke, and after the first few seconds of that Dr. Dinkins growled and turned off the speaker.

"They're Stodgers," Ben observed. Short, wide creatures with three flexible arms, a narrow head with a vertical mouth slit, atop a rounded body. Like many Visitors, they wore clothing with pockets crammed with objects—in this case vests that covered only their upper halves, leaving their hairy, stubby tripod legs exposed.

They behaved much as human tourists might. Standing at their table—the chairs wouldn't fit them—they looked at menus, discussed choices, ordered by pointing at the menu for a nervous waiter. The film cut to the chef ringing a bell to say the order was ready, the food being delivered—several plates—and the Stodgers sampling from them with obvious relish, bobbing up and down and chatting with gestures. When they left, the camera zoomed in on the small pewter-colored bar of metal they'd left on the table.

After an hour or so of them asking to have the film run back to review parts, the projectionist they'd borrowed from the film school started to complain.

"If you could stop it on one frame," Ben said, "we wouldn't have to repeat it so many times."

The projectionist started to rewind the reel. "If I do, the heat of the lamp will burn it up."

"Then run it as slowly as you can," Dr. Dinkins said. "We'll look for frames we need to get prints of. Wendy, you time it. Ben and I will call out when we see something interesting. Note it down with the time, so we can find it again in the darkroom."

Right, Wendy thought as she walked to Dinkins' office for the stopwatch. The men get to say what's interesting, and the woman copies the information down, though the film was *her* discovery.

•　　　•　　　•

Dinkins pointed at one of the stills tacked to his office wall. "I don't think those are just gestures. Some are sign language." He scratched the white stubble on his chin. "I think that's a variant of the verb 'to go,' for instance. Insofar as they have verbs."

Wendy shut the door and looked around for a place to set down a bag of Big Boy burgers, but every square inch was covered with carefully arranged photo prints. "I suppose they don't like to talk with their mouths full," she said. "You two could learn from their example." She took her sandwich and passed the bag to Ben, who dug inside eagerly.

Wendy folded back the wrapper to prevent drips, then wandered around looking at the photographs. None of them had slept for over a day, and she was feeling light-headed. "This sign is similar to the sign for 'good'. Larry's doing it after eating a lot of the Reuben sandwich." Wendy had nicknamed the Visitors after her niece and nephew.

"Ben will look at that," Dinkins mumbled around a mouthful of tuna sandwich. "I'd like you to catalog the contents of their pockets."

That was a hopeless task. How was she supposed to identify bulges in fabric? "I know more of their languages than Ben does, he's the gadget man, and it is my discovery, after all."

"Now, Wendy, we're all on the same team here. You have a better eye for detail than Ben does, so it makes sense to have you analyze the peripheral things and catalog what you can. It all contributes to the complete picture."

So, Wendy thought, I'm better than Ben in all the relevant ways, but I should do the less important part of the work. But there was no point in saying so. "Right," she said, with a tight little smile. She picked up a stack of photos at random. "I'll start with these."

•   •   •

When Wendy woke, she had to peel off a photo that had adhered to her cheek. She used her makeup mirror to check for marker ink on her face. On her way to the restroom, she met Ben coming up the stairs with a coffee pot and mugs on a tray. "Oh my God." She stepped out of his way. "If some of that is for me, you're forgiven."

Ben looked puzzled. "What for?"

"Never mind. Just pour me some with a lot of sugar. I'll be right back."

When she returned, she found Ben poring over her stack of prints, the best shots she'd found of every bulge, pin, cord, and piece of equipment that festooned the Stodgers' vests. He handed her a cup. "Anything interesting?"

"Susan can't read English well." Wendy took a sip of too-hot coffee, then another, then added another two teaspoons of sugar. "She looks at her menu through a lens she keeps in this pocket. I think it's a translating device."

"Couldn't she just be near-sighted?"

"She never uses it to consult her wrist device." She refused to call it a "Dick Tracy Radio" as Ben did. "The symbols on that are tiny."

"Wouldn't I like to get my hands on that lens! Then we could do some real translating!"

"Yes. Except that, like every other device anyone's ever swiped off them, it wouldn't work for us."

"True." Ben flipped to another photo. "What's this that you circled, in Larry's pocket?"

"It only appears in a few frames, as they turn to leave. A rectangular object with markings on the outside. This little bit near the top is all that's visible, and it has part of a circle and some slanted stripes, with maybe the top quarter inch of a row of symbols."

"Any idea what it is?"

"Not yet. Too bad it's not Technicolor. Then in this frame, this pocket maybe holds two hover globes."

"Dr. Dinkins has spoken to someone at Fox Movietone, and they promised to send over all the original film."

"Excellent."

"And he's asked our clipping service to look especially for any other news about this pair. It's great that we have some Visitors doing something comprehensible for a change. We should go through the files of past clippings to see where they've been. Maybe we can predict where they'll show up next."

Maybe. Wendy at least could predict which of them would be given the task of looking through old clippings.

•   •   •

Wendy arrived in Hilbert for the Cheese Derby on the 8:17 AM bus. Farm people rise early, so there were already plenty of locals patronizing the booths. She wandered, looking for members of her family.

Greta, the twins, and Tad were together beside the entertainment tent. Tad surveyed the fairgrounds with a proprietorial air from atop a barrel. His beagle, Charley, got up as she approached, greeting her to the limit of his red leather leash. Greta's attention was taken up by the twins, also on leashes, though theirs were improvised from rope. Based on the staining of their faces and coveralls, little Larry and Susan had already had both snow cones and chocolate.

Tad smiled serenely and directed her to a second barrel. "So glad you could make it. I was afraid your school project would keep you away."

Wendy leaned against her barrel, and the dog sniffed around her feet. "I had a break. We're waiting for more film to look at." She leaned over to rumple Charley's floppy ears.

Greta picked up Susan and jiggled her to stop her crying. "Tad said you're studying Visitors who go to diners? What do you hope to learn from that?"

"More of their languages."

"What's the point? They speak English, don't they?"

"Some of them. But you never really understand a culture until you can speak the language. Besides, we'd like to be able to tell what they're saying to each other that they might not want us to hear."

Larry, seeing Susan getting attention, started to whine and tug at his mom's skirt, so Wendy picked him up.

"Is their language especially hard?"

"They have a few different ones. They all have weird grammar. The main problem is they aren't willing to teach it to us, and most of what we have is writing. Without something like the Rosetta Stone, it's impossible to figure out text without clues what it means."

Greta set Susan down, and the toddler immediately became interested in a bug. "And you think it'll help to watch them eat?"

"Yes, because we know what sorts of things people say to each other while eating. If we can predict where they'll show up next, we'll be there with cameras and tape machines."

"Any idea yet where that'll be?" Tad said.

"Not much. This pair only shows up in the USA, which is odd since other Visitors don't seem to pay any attention to borders. It looks like they might be following major roads, though I can't think why they should, since their saucers can land anywhere. I need more data points."

"Well, this is fascinating," Greta said, "but I see John over there, and I plan to make him play ring toss to win stuffed toys for the twins and a nice clock for me. Find us when the concert starts; we brought a picnic, and there's plenty."

"Thanks, I will."

"As for me," Tad said, "I'd like to hear more, but my smoke break is over. Want to come along and help me set up for the Cheese Queen pageant?"

"I'd just bore you complaining about my colleagues. I thought I'd try my hand at that dunking booth."

He waved a hand. "Please sample the delights of our little jubilee. Can I throw your bag in the trunk?"

Wendy handed over the bag and gave the dog a final scratch between the shoulder blades. She didn't know who would be sitting in the booth awaiting a soaking, but she planned, as she hurled each baseball, to envision Dr. Dinkins' face on that unfortunate person. It would sharpen her aim.

After venting her frustrations, Wendy also spoiled her lunch with ice cream and funnel cake. Then she found a shady bench on which to sip a Coke and watch the athletic contests occurring on a nearby lawn.

The competitors in the Egg and Spoon race displayed a few different strategies, ranging from the mad dash of optimism to varying degrees of caution. The race was dominated by two competitors—a rangy young man who adopted a bent-legged posture to minimize joggling while using his long legs to cover ground, and a pigtailed girl of about eleven years who adopted the mad dash strategy, her egg rocking precariously as she charged past less fortunate competitors whose eggs decorated the lawn, eventually edging out her long-legged rival.

At lunch, Greta handed out generous portions of tuna noodle casserole, blackberry cobbler, and lemonade from a thermos bottle. Afterward, having seen everything of interest, Wendy walked to the town's one hotel and found a comfortable chair near a window in the quiet lobby, where she read news clippings and journal articles until she judged it was nearly time for her brother's magic show.

Tad had entertained them, as a child, with more skill at sleight of hand than the usual amateur. He'd only improved since then, and his 'patter' was rapid, smooth, and entertaining. The volunteers he brought up on stage were suitably bewildered when cards they'd chosen mysteriously showed up in their pockets, and items they'd thought secure on their persons ended up in the magician's hat. It might be merely the bias of a loving sister, but Wendy thought he upstaged the pageant which was to follow. Tad took his final bow to loud applause. As the master of ceremonies came out to introduce the contestants, he slipped around back to take the seat Wendy had saved for him.

Wendy complimented him on his performance, but Tad waved that aside. "I heard something on the radio which will interest you," he said. "The Visitors have just purchased land in New Mexico. Lots of it."

•　　　•　　　•

The nearest phone booth was inside the bus station. Wendy called Professor Dinkins at home.

"I've heard," he said, cutting her off. "The commander at Holloman Air Force Base called me, in fact. He's been ordered to keep an eye on their activities, and wanted my advice." Dinkins sounded inordinately pleased about this. "The Visitors have cordoned off the site with a ring of hover globes, and they're building something. I have to get down there and try and talk with them."

"Excellent! I can be ready to go in ..." Wendy calculated the amount of time it would take to get back to her apartment, throw a few things in a travel bag, arrange for a neighbor to water her plants. "About an hour and a half."

"Oh, but I need you here. Someone has to cover my Cultural Anthropology course."

The ET Studies department was too new, and had too little material, to have its own courses, so Dinkins still taught classes for his old department.

"Henry, d-darn it! It's summer! There are only five students and, what, three more class sessions? Anyway, Ben can handle that. You need your best linguist on this trip."

"I'm sorry, but I don't think Ben's qualified to teach that course. He only took it himself last term. It has to be you. I can manage the linguistics angle in New Mexico; I need Ben for his technical knowledge. Plus, I'll be working with the brass."

And they'll find your assistant more credible if it's a man, Wendy filled in. "I see. Well, there's no rush my getting back to town, then."

"You needn't take that tone. You can join us in New Mexico after finals. This will be a long-term project. I'll leave my class notes in your box, and once I arrive, I'll call with a number where I can be reached."

"Happy travels," Wendy said, hanging up with unnecessary force.

•   •   •

"I could've taken the bus," Wendy said.

"Nonsense." Tad waited for her to get in, closed the car door, and walked around to the driver's side. "It sounds like you'll be very busy, so when else will we have an opportunity to visit?"

"You'll still be able to visit me in Appleton for a few weeks at least."

"You're not going to New Mexico immediately?"

"No, but to look at the bright side, at least now I have the diner project all to myself. Maybe I can get a paper out of it."

"Have you made any progress with that?"

"Not really. Today I found news stories about two more diners that had visits. Maybe there'll be a pattern when I add them to the map. It looks like the visits are always six days apart. I might call a few more of the places and ask them questions, but it's hard to get anything useful over the phone."

The sun was finally setting on the long summer day; Tad turned on the headlamps. "It won't be the same here without you."

"I keep telling you, you should leave anyway."

"I will before long, but still. Everything's changing." Tad watched the road. "Why don't we take a trip? Just you and me?"

"I could, next weekend. Where do you want to go?"

"I don't care. Are any of your diners near enough to drive to?"

"There's one a couple of hours south. For a person driving at a normal speed, that is, instead of creeping along as you're doing now."

"There are deer on this stretch at night. All right, we make it a day trip. Or if you have time, we could spend a night in Madison."

"There's another diner in Mt. Horeb, so maybe we could."

"It's a deal. And if I spend Friday night on your couch, we can get an early start."

"Oh, really? Are you sure it's because of that, or could it be that you expect me to make crab croquettes for dinner?"

Tad shrugged. "If I'm to be your research assistant, a laborer is worthy of his hire."

•　　　•　　　•

The name hadn't led her to expect much, but The Grease Pit Restaurant in West Allis was actually sparkling clean, with black and white tile walls in a checker pattern, and an auto-racing theme. Wendy and Tad sat at a chrome-edged table, on faux-leather stools.

"We must be near a speedway," Wendy said.

Tad nodded. "There is one in town."

"I'm surprised you know that."

"What do you think men talk about in bars? Hunting, politics, their amatory conquests, but sports most of all."

"You go to bars?" Her little brother. It was a distressing picture.

"Sometimes. Often enough that I've heard them speak of coming down to see races here." Tad looked up as a waitress appeared, a woman in her late forties in a pink-and-white checked dress which must be a uniform. "Is it too early for the bacon and tomato sandwich?"

"No, sir, we can do that."

"Plain burger, please." Wendy handed the menu back. "And after you get the order in, will you sit and talk with us for a while?"

The waitress looked surprised, but shrugged. "I suppose. So long as nobody else comes in." The only other customers were two men in stained overalls, wolfing down large, late breakfasts.

By the time she returned, Wendy had opened her satchel and spread photos out across the tabletop. When the waitress saw them, comprehension dawned. "Oh, it's about *them*?"

"We're from Lawrence University in Appleton, and we study them. Wendy Wilks, Tad Wilks. Were you here when they came?"

"I'm Veronica, Ronnie to my friends. Yes, I served them myself. It was lunchtime, so we had two other girls working, but they were afraid to come out. Of course, the place pretty much cleared out anyway. One old gent wanted to shoot them, but my husband talked him out of it. We're the owners; he cooks."

"Can you tell whether it was the same pair as in these photos?"

Ronnie sifted through the pictures carefully. "Can't say for certain. It was the same kind of critters, dressed the same. It's a disgrace the way they go about in public with their bits hanging down. But they did seem to enjoy their meal."

"I understand they're good tippers," Tad said.

"Rafe and me held on to the bar they left. We hear it's valuable, but ain't figured out yet where best to sell it. Once he's done your sandwiches, I can get him out here too, if you like."

"Yes, please." Wendy pointed to spots she'd circled on the photos. "We want to know what they were carrying in all these pockets, whether they took anything out, and what they did with it."

Ronnie sifted through the photos, stopping at one that showed the Visitor Susan using its lens. "This here lorgnette thing. My grandma had one like that. The little one used it to look at the menu, same as it's doing here."

"Did the other one read a menu too?"

"Yeah, but he just looked at it. He did take out a round thing, about this big, like a yoyo without a string. I didn't see from which pocket. He played with it a little. Twisted it, like."

Wendy pulled out a thin binder titled "Gizmo Guide," and flipped to a sketch of a flat ovoid with markings on it, and a line around its edge. Ben had facetiously labeled it, "Captain Rocket Secret Decoder Ring (actual size)," even though it wasn't ring shaped and probably not used for decoding. "One of these?"

"Could be. The top and bottom turned in different directions."

Wendy made a note. "All right. Anything else?"

"It was several weeks back. Can I look through that book?"

While Ronnie looked through the Gizmo binder, her husband brought their food out himself. He was a large man with graying hair, whose skin showed the effects of lots of time outdoors. Since their table was covered with photos and papers, he set the food on the adjacent one, and leaned over Ronnie's shoulder. "Is this the same pair?" he asked.

"We believe so," Tad said. "What do you remember?"

"I was mostly back in the kitchen." He pointed to a photo that showed the rectangular object peeping from the pocket of Larry's vest. "Don't that look familiar, Ronnie?"

Ronnie pulled the picture closer. "You think our critters had one, too?"

"No, I just think I seen one before. Y'all don't have a better picture of this?"

"Unfortunately, no." Wendy handed him a magnifying glass, but she knew the image wasn't clear enough to make out much more detail. Perhaps the original film would be sharper.

The bell over the door signaled the arrival of more customers. "Let me think on it while I see what those gentlemen want."

After they'd eaten, paid, and were ready to leave, Wendy handed Ronnie a note with her phone number on it. "In case you remember anything else."

In the car, Wendy consulted the state road map to find the best way to Madison, but as they were pulling out of the parking lot Tad slammed the brakes, skidding to a stop on the gravel drive.

Wendy put her hand on the dash. "What's the trouble?"

"The cook is running after us."

Tad backed into the lot, and Rafe ran up to the passenger window, grinning and waving something. "I got it!" He handed the object through the window. "This is what it had in its pocket."

It was a thin paperback book, old and beat up, the cover coming loose. *Diner Rover*, by Myron K. Engels, with a cover photo of a hamburger and shake on a table beside a tattered road map.

"I don't understand," Wendy said. "They left this book behind?"

"No, this is my copy. See, I dogeared our page." Rafe reached in to open the book. There was a short review describing The Grease Pit, mentioning the car parts mounted on the walls, talking about foods the author had liked, the pleasures of eavesdropping on race car drivers, and the prompt and friendly service.

"The Visitors must have their own copy," Tad said. He pointed to a different review on the facing page.

"Look, isn't that the place they stopped in Mt. Horeb? That's wild!"

Wendy was speechless. She flipped to the back, finding an index sorted by name, and another by city. The place in New York, Soderberg's Deli, was there. Wendy dove into her bag for her master list of dates and places, and scanned the index, matching more names. "My g-gosh! Is this how they plan their visits?"

Rafe leaned his elbows on the car door, grinning. "It's sorted in order of when the author went there. He's a nice guy, but kind of a nut. Drives around and stops wherever catches his eye. He was here early on, about six years ago, so we're near the front. He sent us this copy when it was published."

Wendy leafed through. The book was divided into sections, each pertaining to one drive across country, east-west or north-south. "The Visitors couldn't have gone to all these places in order. There are too many."

"If it's a few years old, a lot of them might have closed," Tad said, "what with the war. And maybe they skip around. How do you suppose they got a copy?"

"Oh," Wendy said distractedly, "they have lots of books. They bought the Carnegie Library in Muncie, Indiana. Hauled the whole thing off into space. Let's park, go inside and figure this out. Is there a bookstore near here? We might need the latest edition."

•　　　•　　　•

The young man who entered the Ribs of Fire Barbeque Extravaganza of Kalamazoo was short and muscular, with curly black hair and a nose that had been broken at least once. He took a look around and came straight to Wendy's booth, extending a hand. "You must be Wendy Wilks. Dr. Tom Poderman, call me Tom."

Wendy shook his hand—he had a firm grip, but didn't crunch her knuckles. She gestured to the seat across from her, and he threw down his backpack and sat, loose-limbed. "What would you like me to tell my guys? We brought our gear in a panel truck, and we figure to set it up around the saucer after they land and get out, so we can measure what happens when they leave."

Wendy relaxed a little. Tom hadn't charged in and tried to take over; he might be easy to work with. "Good plan. Please tell them to stay out of sight, under trees and some distance away, until the saucer lands and the Visitors are clear of it. They've been known to stay away if it looks like someone's waiting for them."

Tom nodded. "Where do you expect them to land, and when?"

"Between thirty minutes and three hours from now, probably in the parking lot outside or the vacant lot down the road, but possibly up to four blocks away. Either they like to walk sometimes, or don't know exactly where the restaurants are. I assume you have someone on watch, so you can drive your truck to the site?"

"I do."

"Did you bring a camera so we can film them in here?"

Tom pulled a smaller bag from his pack, and unzipped it to show a handheld Arriflex movie camera. "As instructed. I'll have to work it myself, I'm afraid. It was a condition of my borrowing it."

"That's fine with me. When I use a camera, I'm doing well if I don't end up with a picture of my knee.

But don't you want to be operating your equipment outside?"

"And miss a chance to see real live aliens up close? No, indeed. The boys know how to do the job."

"I hope you're not disappointed. I'm only 80 percent sure this is their next stop."

"Good enough odds for me. If this comes off, I'll owe you. I've got three different theories about how the saucers fly, and even if we rule out all three today, that's progress. I'm just surprised you didn't bring in people from your own department on this. Pleased, but surprised."

Wendy snorted. "They're busy with more important things."

"Ah, they're in New Mexico? Your prof must have a lot of pull. When the department secretary called to say there was someone in town from the Extraterrestrial Studies Department at Lawrence, I was amazed there was such a thing. How'd you get it set up in less than a year?"

Wendy spotted Tad emerging from the kitchen with a tray for another table, and signaled him to come over. "A large grant from the Department of the Army helped. Before the Visitors came, Professor Dinkins was a crackpot anthropologist writing papers about the hypothetical capabilities and practices of alien species."

"Ah. And then suddenly he was the foremost authority on a subject of vital interest to the military. Yes, that would help to expedite matters."

"He really is a remarkable man," Wendy said.

"And yet, I sense that's a somewhat grudging compliment."

Tad showed up, pad in hand. "May I get you something else? The ribs are exceptionally tasty."

She wasn't sure whether Tad would like working as a waiter, but *playing* waiter for a day was clearly another matter. Wendy pushed her empty Coke glass toward him, feeling a mischievous urge. "Do they come with frim-fram sauce?"

"We don't get a lot of call for it, miss, but I'll see whether there's any. I know we're out of shafafa. What about you, sir?"

Tom looked at him suspiciously, then at Wendy. "You two are related."

Wendy laughed. "This is my brother Tad, here by special arrangement for one day only. I need his skills. Tad, Dr. Tom Poderman."

Tad bowed. "I was serious about the ribs. I sneaked a taste and they're most excellent."

Tom set the menu aside. "I'll try a small order, but I also need something for my five guys outside, something quick that won't drip sauce on my expensive equipment."

Tad pursed his lips. "This isn't a restaurant that serves tidy food, but I'll see what I can manage."

"Thanks, bud. I need to go give them their instructions. Will you bring the food out to them when it's ready?"

"I will."

"And salad for me," Wendy called after him.

In a few minutes Tom returned, carrying an Army surplus two-way radio the size and shape of a brick. "Test, one two," he said into it as he sat. "Over."

Test okay. Over.

"Acknowledged, over and out." He set the radio aside as Tad set a basket before him. "Whoa, that's the small order?"

"That's the medium order. I heard you say small, but I know this woman well, and since she ordered salad, I guarantee she'll end up filching some of your food. She can't help it; it's an involuntary reflex."

"Tad, you're embarrassing me."

"The truth shall set you free, sis. Free to feast on tasty ribs, in this case."

Tom pushed the basket closer to the center of the table, unsuccessfully hiding a smile. "Please help yourself. This really is too much. If we might be here for hours, I'll have to pace myself."

•　　•　　•

They were there for hours; a little over two hours, discussing Wendy's family and choice of major, Tom telling funny stories about his service in the Navy. He listened to her explanation of the theorized three main dialects of Eklatt without any sign of wishing to escape. Wendy was almost sorry when the radio crackled to life, a tense voice announcing, *They're here. Hovering over the vacant lot.*

Tom waited for a second, then pressed the mic button. "Over?"

Sorry. They're coming down. Um, over.

"Get out of sight, casual-like, copy? Over."

Roger, over and out.

Wendy, heart pounding, stood to address the other patrons in the restaurant, which had filled up a bit. "Attention, please, everyone. The Visitors are about to arrive. You were all already told, but I want to say again, no Visitor has ever harmed anyone who wasn't attacking them, and this pair has eaten peacefully in many restaurants without causing trouble. If you need to leave now, please go quietly out the back."

Nobody left. No doubt a lot of them were here because word had gotten around about the expected visit. Tad nipped out from the back and removed the "Reserved" sign from the table they'd chosen for its optimal camera angle, and over which they'd suspended a microphone, hidden in the light fixture. The cord ran into the kitchen, to a steel-tape recorder Wendy had "borrowed" from the psychology lab at Lawrence. Tom got the camera out and aimed it at the door.

The next few minutes seemed like hours. Wendy held her breath as a shadow fell across the glass, and the door chime rang. Then they were inside. A chill ran down her spine. Beside Wendy, the camera whirred to life. Everybody turned to look at the arrivals. Tad hurried toward the Visitors, acting nervous, and she wondered how much of that was really an act. Despite the assurances she'd just given, her stomach was doing flips from being in the same room with her first live aliens.

Tad gestured them to the prepared table, and they went along, thank God. The smaller one, Susan, paused and looked around at the crowd, said something to Larry. Larry looked around too, then flashed signs back, in which Wendy only caught the sign for "irrelevant."

"They're not used to being expected," Tom murmured. "There's usually some panic."

That was probably right. It was awfully quiet in the room, and Wendy would've been a little creeped out herself in that situation. But Larry picked up a menu, and after a moment, Susan followed suit. The crowd started to relax a little, and the visit went much like previous ones. The Visitors ordered many things, ate a little of everything and a lot of potato salad and fried fish, ordered more dishes.

Tad, his hands shaking, at one point knocked over a glass of ice water that splashed a little on Susan's vest, reflexively reached out to dab at it with the white towel he'd draped over his arm, then backed off in horror at his own presumption. "Sorry," he whispered. "Sorry. I'll, uh, here, can I hand you the towel?"

For the first time, Larry spoke. "It iss irrelefent. There iss no harm. Brink more water only."

Abashed, Tad retreated into the kitchen. Soon after, the Stodgers gathered themselves, Larry left a metal bar on the table, and they trundled out. The owner of the place watched them go, then grabbed the bar and dropped it into the pocket of his apron.

Wendy began to breathe again. She closed her eyes. "Did you get all that?"

Tom tucked the camera back into the bag. "I think so. I'll get it developed right away. You?"

"We'll see."

Tad came out, leaned near the window to make sure the Visitors weren't returning, and hurried over to Wendy. "The recorder seemed to be working. The dial was jumping, anyway. And I believe you wanted this?"

He dropped it on the table, the treasure she'd come for. The decorative circle and stripes at the top were the same she'd seen before, the cover photo was the same, but the title was in Eklatt script rather than English.

"What is that?" Tom said. "A book?"

Wendy looked at him, eyes sparkling. "That, my friend, is the Rosetta Stone. The Eklatt edition of *Diner Rover* by Myron K. Engels."

"Wait, you stole this from them? How did they not notice?"

Tad drew himself up. "I didn't steal it. It was an ... involuntary trade. I exchanged it for a copy of the English edition."

Wendy stood. "Still, they'll notice eventually, so let's clear out before they do. I have a lot of work to do."

Tom stood also, hoisting his pack. "I have a little homework of my own, but could we get together again before you leave town?"

Wendy touched his arm. "Tom, I enjoyed our conversation, and I'd love to see you again, but we're leaving this minute. I need my books and my office, and there's not a moment to lose. Tad, take the microphone down; I'll pack up the tape machine."

•   •   •

Wendy was met at the airfield without ceremony; an Army corporal took her two bags and dropped them into the back of a battered, dusty jeep. "Jeez, that's heavy."

"I brought a few books."

"Everybody's out at the site," he said, handing her a pair of wireframe sunglasses. "You'll want these. Want to go straight there, or drop this stuff off in your quarters first?"

"Straight there, please."

Wendy held her hat on her head as they cruised along at unreasonable speed, then bounced over a badly washboarded dirt road for miles. She could see the Visitors' base long before they arrived; the construction appeared complete, the multiple towers she'd seen in photos now extended upward to merge into a blobby shape with horizontal bands of red and white, shimmering in the sunlight. The jeep pulled up beside a group of Quonset huts at least a mile from the huge alien structure. "The perimeter is about a hundred yards that way," he said. "Your professor fellow is usually in hut number three."

Dr. Dinkins was indeed in number three, he and Ben looking sunburned and sleep-deprived as they sorted through stacks of photos. "Ah, good, you're here," Dinkins said. "How did things go with my class?"

"Routinely. I brought back the final examinations for you to grade."

Dinkins grimaced. "That may have to wait a while. We're quite busy, and you will be also. Anything interesting going on back home?"

"No … all very boring. I made some progress on that diner project." She didn't mention that her first version of an Eklatt-English lexicon and grammar was in the satchel on her shoulder. Wendy leaned over the worktable, glancing over what were mostly telephoto shots of the stages of construction, Visitors and machines wandering around their … their campus, she supposed you could call it. "Before I get started, I'd like to see it in person."

"Certainly." Dinkins waved. "Just walk that way, you can't miss it. When you reach the edge, you'll know."

As promised, the border of the Visitors' property was obvious. Crews in Army and Air Force uniforms clustered around the perimeter, using cameras, radio dishes, and other devices that Tom Poderman would've recognized. On the way in, they'd driven past a perimeter of guards facing out. These guards were facing in. She walked past them, toward a row of wooden stakes. There was a shimmer in the air that as she approached, resolved into thousands of golden hover globes in rapid motion. They must have sensed her approach, because the area ahead became denser with them, a swarm of giant, silent golden bees. One step closer, and several of them froze in position blocking her path, absolutely steady in midair.

She turned to look at an Army man working on one of the monitoring devices. "Can I touch them?"

He looked up, distractedly, then shrugged. "They ain't hurt nobody yet. They just don't move out of the way."

Her heart pounding, Wendy rested her hand on one of the globes. It was about two inches across, warm, body temperature. She pushed. There was absolutely no give.

She stepped back, looking around. It was worthless land the Visitors had bought, scrubby desert with no trees except the occasional cactus. What she wanted was a stick, but there was none in sight. Except ...

"Hey, don't do that," the technician said. "They told us not to move those stakes."

"I'll put it back in a moment." Wendy turned her back on the globes. This probably wouldn't work, but it was worth a try. Everything showed the Visitors were curious. Novelty seekers. Some of them had a sense of humor, of sorts. Could she be interesting enough to win an audience?

She'd spent the flight planning her message. She wanted something with a few unusual words, a little bit of complicated syntax, to make it look like she knew the language better than she really did. And she'd done the best she could; she should stop doubting herself and just do it.

She held the stick poised, then began to draw Eklatt symbols in the hard, sandy soil. Large, in case the globes were far-sighted.

To enter allow me, she wrote, *for talk with enthusiasts of cuisine. The ingredients and preparations most sublime I know.* That, at least, was what she hoped it said. She looked at the technician, who was staring at her, and made a last-second decision to add a diacritical over "me" to turn it into "me alone". And she stepped aside to let the globes have a look, pushing the stake back into the ground where she'd gotten it.

Wendy felt sure the Visitors could see what the globes could see, if they chose. But was anyone watching, and would they care? She waited a few minutes in the hot sun, then sighed. It had been worth a try. She turned away, preparing herself mentally for the work before her— reading reports, writing reports, evaluating tapes and photos, attending meetings where nobody would be interested in what she had to say. But the look on the technician's face made her spin back around.

The globes had shifted, creating a round tunnel. Wendy's heart pounded, and quickly, before she could change her mind or the man could stop her, she wiped out the message with swipes of her shoe, took three quick strides to the border and another two into the tunnel.

"Hey!" the technician shouted, and there were other shouts from nearby, and pounding of booted feet. Wendy looked back over her shoulder. The globes had closed in behind her, blocking the path of two men who'd run up to the edge. Blocking her also, but the Visitors wouldn't stop her from leaving if she chose.

At least, she hoped not.

"You have to come out of there," one man said, angry or afraid or both. Three more ran up behind him.

"I won't stay too long. I just want to chat with some ... people." Or write them notes, anyway. She held up her notebook. "Please assure Dr. Dinkins that I'll carefully record all my observations. I feel certain I'll be perfectly safe."

Well, almost certain. She took a deep breath, and walked toward her future.

•   •   •

Tad was awakened just before dawn by a tapping at his window. Woodpecker, he thought, and turned over. But then it came again, rapping out "shave and a haircut." Had someone put a ladder up to his window to knock on the glass? Who, and why? Nobody was visible out there, so he threw the covers aside and went to look down at the yard, scratching his chest through his pajamas.

Nobody. But then there was another tap and he jumped back, finally looking up to see the golden sphere, a small cutout against the brightening sky. It darted to the bottom of the window and bobbed up and down.

Like hell he was going to open the window to that thing.

The ball jiggled, giving every sign of impatience. Then a hole opened in its top and a white finger extended from it. No, not a finger. A folded-up piece of paper. There was just light enough for him to read his name on the outside, in a familiar handwriting.

He flipped the catch and raised the window, reaching tentatively toward the note, then making a grab for it. The sphere didn't react while he unfolded the paper, hands trembling, and read.

Dearest Taddlywinks,

Having a wonderful time. Wish you were here. Since you're not, however ...

Last time I was in town, Big Mike's had a "Help Wanted" sign in the window. Go get that job, and make

*sure you're working at lunchtime next Thursday. And
see to it they have fresh apple and gooseberry pies then,
because I've been talking those up.*

Love, W

ABOUT THE AUTHOR

Tyler Tork is a longtime fan and writer of science fiction and fantasy, with three books in print, another out of print, and more in the queue. After retiring from a career in computers, he writes, creates art, and manages the worldwide map of Free Little Art Galleries.

YOU MIGHT ALSO ENJOY

FLAWLESS
by J. Scott Coatsworth

Grayson Eck's life is a drag—in all the best possible ways. He's perfectly happy working in the belt alone as a wildcatter, prospecting asteroids by ... well, not exactly by day.

HAMM AND MEGS
by Gary Battershell

When Megan decided to go on a camping trip with her two college roommates, she had no idea that she would find herself involved in an alien plot to conquer Earth.

LITTLE GREEN MEN
by Curtis Bass

In an orbiting craft, Cooper has a front row seat to the first manned mission to Mars. Their landing is perfect until one crew member claims they are being watched by indigenous creatures.

Available in digital and trade paperback editions from
Water Dragon Publishing
waterdragonpublishing.com